by Ron Roy
illustrated by Timothy Bush

A STEPPING STONE BOOK™

Random House New York

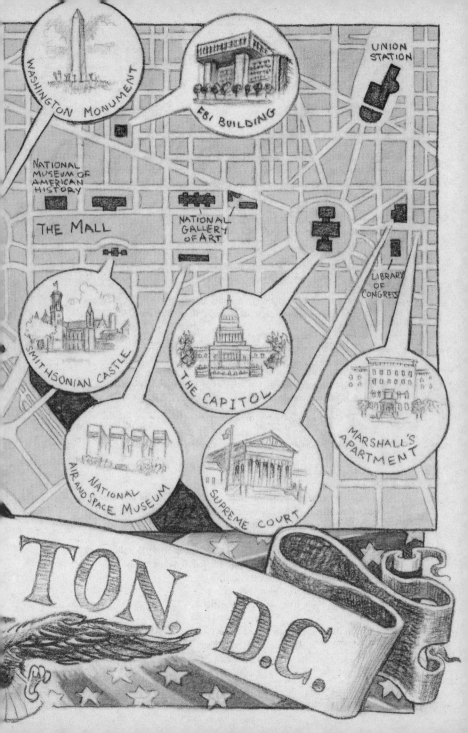

For Simon and Tansy
—R.R.

Photo credits: p. 88, courtesy of the Library of Congress.

Text copyright © 2008 by Ron Roy
Illustrations copyright © 2008 by Timothy Bush

Visit us on the Web!
www.steppingstonesbooks.com
www.randomhouse.com/kids

Educators and librarians, for a variety of teaching tools, visit us at
www.randomhouse.com/teachers

Library of Congress Cataloging-in-Publication Data
Roy, Ron.
The election-day disaster / by Ron Roy ; illustrated by Timothy Bush.
— 1st ed.
    p.   cm. — (Capital mysteries ; 10)
"Stepping Stone book."
Summary: When doctored photographs of the President of the United States appear after an innocent Halloween party, his stepdaughter KC and her friend Marshall have to find the culprit in order to save the President's chances for re-election.
ISBN 978-0-375-84805-6 (pbk.) — ISBN 978-0-375-94805-3 (lib. bdg.)
[1. Elections—Fiction. 2. Presidents—Fiction. 3. Washington (D.C.)—Fiction. 4. Mystery and detective stories.]
I. Bush, Timothy, ill. II. Title.
PZ7.R8139Ek 2008   [Fic]—dc22   2007048208

Printed in the United States of America
10 9 8 7 6 5 4 3 2 1   First Edition

Contents

1
Halloween Trouble

"Marshall, I don't think you should be up in that tree," KC said. She glanced down at the small sign stuck in the White House lawn. "This tree was planted by President Truman. It's very valuable!"

"I'm not hurting it." Marshall's voice came from the branches. "I'm just making my spiderweb look more spooky."

KC and her friend Marshall were in the White House rose garden. It was Halloween, and in an hour, the garden would be filled with kids and grown-ups in costumes. Even though the leaves were changing color, it was warm for the end of October. Kids wouldn't need their hats and jackets to go out trick-or-treating.

President Zachary Thornton was KC's stepfather. Since KC's mom had married the president, KC and her mother had been living in the White House.

"It already looks spooky," KC said. She glanced around the garden at the jack-o'-lanterns, "ghosts" made out of sheets, and fake tombstones.

Marshall dropped to the ground. He was dressed as a tarantula. To make the legs, he'd stuffed long black socks and tied them to his black T-shirt and black jeans. He'd drawn a spider face on his own, using face paint.

Marshall Li was an animal lover. But he especially liked creatures with six or more legs. His pet tarantula, Spike, lived in a cage next to his bed.

"How does it look?" he asked, pointing up into the tree. His "spiderweb" was really white knitting yarn he'd gotten from his mother. He had strung the yarn in the tree branches to look like a large web.

"Pretty nice," KC admitted. "And the web goes with my costume."

"You're not coming as a spider, too!" Marshall yelped.

"No, I'm coming as Wilbur," KC said.

"Who's Wilbur?"

"He's the pig in *Charlotte's Web*," KC said. "My favorite book."

"I hate to break the news," Marshall said, "but in the book, Charlotte built a spiderweb, not a pig web."

"I didn't say Wilbur sat in the web," KC said. "Besides, how would you know? You only read Spider-Man comics."

"I saw the movie." Marshall grinned.

"Sweet web, Marsh," a voice said. It was almost dark in the rose garden, and the voice made KC jump.

Simon Tansy jogged toward the tree. He was the nephew of Yvonne, the president's maid. Simon was visiting Yvonne for a few days.

"Thanks, Simon," Marshall said. "Where's your costume?"

Simon winked. "Somewhere," he said. Simon was thirteen and thin, and had the yellowest blond hair KC had ever seen. He puffed out his chest. "I'm coming as Arnold Schwarzenegger."

"You can't!" KC said. "Everyone has to be some kind of animal. It says so on your invitation."

"I know," Simon said. He tugged on

KC's long red hair. "I was just yanking your chain. My costume is all ready, and if you think you'll win the costume contest, forget it. It's gonna be mine!"

"What contest?" Marshall said. "No one tells me anything around here!"

"There's a prize for the most creative costume," KC said. "The president and my mom and I are the judges."

"You're a judge?" Simon scoffed. "So you can't win, right?"

"I know that," KC said. She wondered why Simon made her so angry. Since he'd arrived that morning, he'd been nothing but a wise guy.

"She's coming as a pi— Ouch!" Marshall said as KC kicked him on the ankle.

"It's a surprise." KC glared at Marshall.

"Whatever," Simon said, rolling his

eyes. "Your mom told me to tell you to come in and get the apples. You know, for the dunking."

"Okay, thanks," KC said. "I just want to check out the tent first."

Marshall and Simon followed KC to another part of the rose garden. A small tent stood next to the gate. The outside of the tent was decorated with plastic bats, flying witches, and other Halloween stuff.

"Cool," Simon said. "What's this for?"

"Everyone who shows up has to walk through the tent and have a picture taken with their masks off," KC said. "For security. My mom said three marine guards will be here to take their invitations. Then the guests walk out the tent's back door into the party."

"Why? Does the president think there

will be party crashers?" Simon asked.

"He just wants to make sure that only invited guests come," KC explained. "He doesn't want anyone on the grounds who doesn't belong here."

"Our whole class from school is invited!" Marshall said. "And my parents!"

"Great," Simon muttered. "Little kids and grown-ups. I'll have a terrific time!"

Simon pulled out his cell phone and loped away toward the back entrance of the White House.

As Simon went in, Arnold, in his crisp green marine uniform, came out. Arnold was the president's personal guard, and he had become KC and Marshall's friend. He was carrying two large wash buckets.

"Where do these go?" he called to KC. "They're for apple dunking."

"Leave them by the tent," KC said. "I don't know where my mom wants them."

KC and Marshall went into the tent. It was empty except for a chair where the guests would be photographed.

"Who's taking the pictures?" Marshall asked KC. "I thought cameras weren't allowed."

"The president hired a photographer," she said.

By the tent's exit was a basket of red, white, and blue campaign buttons. In the center of each button was the face of President Zachary Thornton. Around his face were the words ZACK IS BACK.

November 4—four days away—was Election Day. KC's stepfather was running for reelection as President of the United States.

"KC, if the president loses the election, where will you guys live?" Marshall asked. "You'd have to move out of the White House, right?"

"He's not going to lose!" KC said. "Don't you ever read the newspapers, Marsh?"

KC planned to be a news anchor-woman after college. She read three newspapers every day and watched the news on TV. She was training herself to notice what was going on everywhere, not just in Washington, D.C.

"I only read Spider-Man comics, re-member?" Marshall said, putting on a goofy face.

"Well, all the polls say my stepfather is ahead of Melrose Jury, the man he's run-ning against," KC said.

"What do you mean, poles?" Marshall asked. "Like fishing poles?"

"No, P-O-L-L-S. Polls are like samples of what people think," KC said. "Whenever there's an election, people get asked who they will vote for. Right now, the president is ahead of Dr. Jury in the polls."

"The president's running against a doctor?" Marshall asked.

"Not a medical doctor," KC said. "Dr. Jury was a college professor before he got into politics."

"And now he wants to be president," Marshall summed up.

KC grinned and pointed to the campaign buttons. "Yeah, but he's not gonna make it, because Zack is back!"

2
No Pictures, Please

An hour later, KC and Marshall were standing next to the two wash buckets filled with water. Apples floated on the surface.

KC had used one of her mom's old pink sweaters to make her Wilbur-the-pig costume. She had stuffed the sweater with a pillow to make her tummy look fat. She wore a pig snout over her nose. Her red hair was tucked under a pink baseball cap with pointy pig ears.

"You look like Miss Piggy," Marshall said.

"Well, I'm not Miss Piggy," KC said. "I'm Mr. Wilbur."

She looked around, checking out all the costumes. Their classmates had masks on, so she couldn't tell who was who.

Some of the adults were standing near the water buckets. Others were lining up kids to play Pin the Wart on the Witch.

"Who's the butterfly?" Marshall asked.

"That's my mom," KC said. "And the president is the lion holding his tail. People keep stepping on it."

"My parents are the two geese," said Marshall. "My mom ripped up a bunch of old pillows to get the feathers."

"The vice president is the ladybug," KC went on. "And Yvonne is the cow."

Marshall pointed to a black gorilla who was pretending to scare kids. "I think that's our teacher, Mr. A," he said.

"Mr. Alubicki is the gorilla?" KC asked.

Marshall nodded. "And your buddy, Simon, is behind the president," he said.

KC stared. Simon was dressed in dark gray long johns. A scrawny gray tail hung from the seat of his pants. Black cardboard ears stuck up from his head over a mask with a pointy nose.

"He looks like a gerbil," KC said, trying not to laugh.

"I think he's supposed to be a kangaroo," Marshall said.

"Who's that?" KC asked. A green monster walked by. Long green sausage-like things hung from the body. The head was a green motorcycle helmet. Strips of green plastic hung down over the legs, almost to the shiny black shoes.

Marshall burst out laughing. "Looks like the Creature from the Black Lagoon!"

KC pointed out a short kid waiting to dunk for an apple. He or she wore a bug mask with a pillowcase for a costume. Black wings sprouted from the shoulders. Every few seconds, the pillowcase lit up. The kid glowed in the dark.

"I think that's Amanda from our class," KC whispered.

"What's she supposed to be?" Marshall asked.

"A firefly," KC said. "Pretty clever!"

It grew darker. Kids dunked for apples. Blindfolded, they tried pinning warts on a paper witch strung between two trees. Cookies and cider were gobbled up.

The president and First Lady arranged a parade around the rose garden. Everyone stumbled along, trying not to step on each other's costumes.

"First prize goes to Amanda Day!" KC's mom announced. "Amanda, your costume is cute and creative and you make a lovely firefly!" Amanda won lunch with the president at the White House. Everyone clapped and whistled.

After Amanda accepted her prize, people began leaving. KC stood by the gate with the president and her mom to say good night to everyone. KC's mom held a basket of wrapped gifts. "Please take one," she said to each guest as they left. "You're all winners!"

The president held the basket of campaign buttons. "Please take one," he joked. "Make me a winner on Tuesday!"

The next morning, KC woke up suddenly. She had heard a shout coming from somewhere in the residence. She jumped up and threw open the door. She heard more loud voices from the kitchen.

Still in her pajamas, KC raced down the hall. The president and her mom and Yvonne were staring at the TV set.

"What is it, Mom?" KC asked.

"Those pictures were on the Internet last night," her mother said. "Now they're all over the news!"

KC focused on the TV screen. It was the *Donny Drum News Hour.* In one of the pictures, the president was shown dunking a boy's head deep into a water bucket. Holding the kid's head down, the president was grinning at the camera.

The other picture was worse. Somebody had put Dr. Melrose Jury's face on the paper witch. President Thornton was pinning a wart on Dr. Jury's nose, and again smiling for the camera.

KC shook her head. "But those things never happened!" she said.

"I think there was a rat at our party last night," the president said. "And that rat wants me to lose this election."

He stood up. "Excuse me," he said. "I have some phone calls to make." He and KC's mom left the kitchen.

KC dialed Marshall's phone number.

"Can you come over?" she asked him when he answered. "We have a disaster!"

Marshall yawned into the phone. "What do you mean, 'we'?" he asked.

"Just come over, okay?"

KC changed out of her pajamas, then sat in the kitchen to wait for Marshall. Simon came in, yawning and holding his cell phone. He poured himself a glass of juice. He smiled at KC, but to her it looked more like a smirk.

"That's too bad about your stepdad," Simon said. But he didn't seem upset.

KC snapped a leash on Natasha, the president's greyhound. They went outside to wait for Marshall.

"Good, you're here!" KC said when Marshall walked up.

"So what's going on?" he asked.

KC took Marshall and Natasha to a sunny bench in the rose garden. The wash buckets and all the Halloween decorations were gone.

"Did you watch TV this morning?" KC asked Marshall. She let go of the leash so Natasha could wander on the lawn.

Marshall was chewing on an apple, so

he shook his head. KC told him about the two pictures that made the president look like a mean person.

Marshall's eyes got big. His face turned red and he started to choke.

"Geez, swallow, will you?" KC said.

He swallowed. "But the president would never dunk a kid," he said. "And I was standing right next to the paper witch. She had a regular old witch's face with a hooked nose and wild hair!"

"Marsh, someone wants to make the president look bad so he'll lose the election," KC said. "Someone at the party took pictures of him, then changed them and put them on the Internet!"

"But no one was supposed to have a camera, remember?" Marshall said.

"Someone did," she said glumly.

"Digital cameras are tiny. Anyone could have hidden one in their costume."

"Wait a minute!" Marshall said. "What about that photographer the president hired, the woman in the tent?"

KC looked at him. "Yeah, her name was Lauren," she said slowly. "Except her camera was big and on a tripod."

"She could have had a small camera, too," Marshall said.

KC shook her head. "Lauren wasn't wearing a costume. We'd have noticed her outside the tent."

"Maybe she did have a costume," Marshall insisted. "You know, we never figured out who was in the green monster costume. Maybe it was Lauren!"

"I guess it's possible," KC agreed. "But that would mean Lauren wants the president to lose the election next week."

"We should go check her out," said Marshall.

"Do you realize what might happen when people see the pictures?" KC said.

Marshall shook his head.

"People will think the pictures are real and that the president did those mean things!" KC said. "The pictures were on the Internet last night. Today they're on TV, and by tomorrow they'll be in every newspaper in the world. The election is three days away!"

"Well, even if it wasn't that photographer, it was definitely someone who was at the party," Marshall said.

"I'm sure none of the kids in our class took those pictures," KC said. "It had to be a grown-up."

"But all the adults were friends of the president." Marshall ticked off names on his fingers. "My parents, Mr. Alubicki, the vice president, and Yvonne. None of them would want to hurt the president!"

"That leaves Lauren, the photographer," KC said quietly.

Marshall jumped up. "KC, maybe the person inside that green monster costume was Dr. Jury!" he said. "Maybe he snuck into the party to take pictures that would make the president look bad!"

KC stared at his big brown eyes, then burst out laughing. "Marsh, I would be willing to bet one million dollars that Dr. Melrose Jury did not crash our party last night," she said.

"So what do we do?" Marshall asked.

"We find the photographer," KC said.

3
Simon Says

KC's mom told her the photographer's name was Lauren Tool. She had a small studio on New York Avenue. Fifteen minutes later, KC and Marshall pushed open the door to her little shop.

KC saw a group of chairs around a low table and a wall of photos. There was a narrow counter with a small door behind it. Below the counter was a glass case filled with cameras for sale.

Lauren Tool was nowhere in sight.

"Check out the cameras," KC whispered. "Some of them are so small I could hide one in my hand."

"Look," Marshall said. He showed KC

a note left on the counter. It said: I'M IN THE DARKROOM. RING THE BELL. LAUREN.

KC pressed the bell next to the note. In a few minutes, Lauren Tool came through the door. She was wearing a plastic apron over jeans and a T-shirt. A picture on her shirt showed a camera with bright eyes and a smiling mouth. Beneath it were the words SAY IT WITH PICTURES.

"Oh, hi," Lauren said when she recognized KC and Marshall. "I told your mom I'd have the pictures tomorrow or the next day."

Lauren Tool was tall. She looked like the kind of woman who played volleyball or basketball. KC flashed back to the green monster costume. Whoever was inside that costume had been tall, too.

"So, what can I do for you?" Lauren asked.

KC thought quickly. Then she asked Lauren if she had seen the news on TV that morning.

Lauren shook her head. "I've been in my darkroom for hours," she said. "Why, what's up?"

KC told her.

"You're kidding me!" Lauren said. She took off her apron and hung it on a hook next to the darkroom door.

"The pictures were awful," KC said. "They made the president look like a terrible person."

"And he's up for reelection," Lauren said. "When people see those pictures, they'll vote for Melrose Jury."

"We need to find out who did it," KC

said. She watched Lauren's face to see if she looked guilty.

"But who could have done such a rotten thing?" Lauren asked. Then her eyes grew wide. "It had to be someone at the Halloween party!"

"We know everyone who came, except for one person," Marshall said. "Someone was wearing a green costume that looked like a weird sea creature."

Again KC studied Lauren's face. Did her expression change when Marshall mentioned the person in the green costume?

"I don't remember anyone like that," Lauren said. She led the kids over to the chairs. "When I finished shooting all the pictures, I counted them. There were twenty-seven. That includes you two kids, plus all your school friends, plus the seven adults."

"That makes twenty-six," KC said. "Nineteen plus seven."

Lauren squinted her eyes, counting silently. "Oh yeah, and that teenager, someone's nephew. He was dressed as a mouse, I think."

"That's Simon Tansy," KC said. "The president's maid is his aunt."

Lauren grinned. "He was kinda cute. Even when I took his picture, he was talking on his cell phone," she said. "Anyway, I got him, too, and that made twenty-seven in all. Trust me, no green sea monster came through the tent to have his picture taken."

Lauren seemed to be telling the truth, KC admitted to herself. Or maybe she was a good actress along with being a good photographer.

"Then he must have snuck in without going through the tent," Marshall said.

"I don't understand how someone dressed like that could have gotten past the two guards," Lauren said. "They stood outside the tent checking invitations."

"Two? But my mom said there were three guards," KC said.

Lauren shrugged. "I only saw two," she said.

Just then KC heard a telephone ring.

"Excuse me," Lauren said. She crossed to the counter and picked up a cell phone. She spoke into it for a few minutes, then came back. "Sorry, but I have to take this call."

KC stood up. "Did you get a good look

at Simon's cell phone?" she asked Lauren.

"Not really. I was focusing on his face," Lauren said. "Why?"

"Maybe his cell phone was also a camera," KC said.

The kids thanked Lauren, then headed back to the White House.

"Do you believe her?" Marshall asked. "I don't. She knows all about cameras, and she had plenty of time to do it."

"Maybe," KC said. "But I still want to talk to Simon. If his cell phone is the kind that can take pictures, he could've put them on the Internet."

"Why would Simon want Melrose Jury to win the election?" Marshall asked. "That would mean you guys would have to leave the White House and his aunt would lose her job."

"I don't know," KC said. "But there was something sneaky about him this morning. He looked like he had a secret."

They found Simon on the couch in the living room. He was staring at his cell phone's small screen. He shut the phone when KC and Marshall came into the room.

The TV was on, and the news was all about the president doing mean things at the White House Halloween party.

A man with blond hair and big teeth was saying: "This is Donny Drum, and I've got your news! Does President Thornton have a mean side that no one has seen before? Why else would he dunk a little kid? Why else would he make fun of Melrose Jury? We don't know the answers to those questions yet. But what we do know is that this will not help the president on voting day. In fact, the latest polls show him slipping. Stay tuned for more on this shocking development at the White House."

KC turned the TV volume down, then she and Marshall sat across from Simon. "Nice cell phone," KC said, nodding at the one Simon held in his hand.

"Thanks," he said. "I got it for my birthday."

"What else can you do with it, besides phone calls and text messages?" asked KC. She noticed that Simon seemed nervous. He was tapping his fingers on the table, and his face had turned pink.

"What do you mean?" Simon asked.

"I mean," KC said, "can you take pictures with it?"

Simon nodded but didn't say anything. He bent down to tie the laces of his running shoes.

KC glanced at Marshall.

"So did you happen to take any pictures at the party last night?" Marshall asked.

By now Simon's face was beet red. "Yeah, a few," he muttered.

"Can we see them?" KC asked.

"I know what you're trying to do!" Simon yelled at KC. "You're trying to blame me for those fake pictures of the president! Well, I didn't do that!"

"Then why did you bring your cell phone with you to the party?" KC asked. "No one was supposed to have a camera."

Simon opened his cell phone and pushed a few buttons. "My teacher told me I have to write a report about visiting the White House," he said. "I wanted pictures for my report, so I snuck my phone in, okay?"

"Were you dressed as a gerbil?" KC asked.

"No, I was Templeton the rat," Simon said. He looked at KC and Marshall. "He's a character in *Charlotte's Web*."

"I know," KC said. "It's my favorite book."

"But I didn't do that stuff!" Simon stabbed a finger toward the TV set. "Even if I knew how to change the pictures, I couldn't have put them on the Internet. My aunt's computer crashed."

KC watched Simon's face. If he was lying, she couldn't tell.

"Did you notice someone wearing a

weird green costume?" KC asked Simon.

"It had stuff hanging on it," Marshall added.

"Yeah, I saw it," Simon said. "In fact, I have pictures."

"You do?" KC said. "Can we see?"

"No problem." Simon fingered a couple buttons, then held the phone so KC and Marshall could see the tiny screen.

Simon clicked through the pictures he had taken last night. Each picture showed kids and grown-ups in costume. "There's your green guy," Simon said.

"Could be a woman," Marshall said. He nudged KC.

"Whatever," Simon said. He paused on a picture of the strange costume.

"What are those long things supposed to be?" Marshall asked.

"I have no clue," KC said. "There are a bunch of them, so they can't be arms."

"Sure they are," Simon said. "The guy—or woman—is an octopus."

Simon clicked ahead to the next picture of the stranger in green. "See, here you can count six dangly arms, plus his two real arms."

"I knew it was some sort of ocean animal," Marshall said. He put his finger on the cell-phone screen. "Maybe that plastic stuff hanging down is supposed to be seaweed."

Simon found another shot of the green octopus. He was standing with some other grown-ups, watching kids dunk for apples. The president was there, too, on his knees next to the washtub.

The next picture showed the green

costume behind the president. They were both watching a blindfolded kid trying to pin a wart on the witch's nose.

KC noticed that the octopus was holding something shiny in one of his real hands.

"Can you make this one bigger?" KC asked.

"A little," Simon said. He pushed a button and the picture enlarged.

"What's in his hand?" KC asked.

"Is he eating something?" Marshall asked.

"No," Simon said. "The dude's got a digital camera!"

4

The Green Monster's Secret

"He's taking a picture!" KC said. "But he's doing it when no one is looking at him. How sneaky!"

KC put her face close to Simon's cell phone and stared at the screen. The green helmet had a plastic visor covering the eyes. KC tried, but she couldn't see the face inside the helmet. Could that be Lauren? KC wondered.

Then she noticed something on one of the fake arms. It looked like writing.

KC put a finger on the picture. "Can you guys see those tiny black letters?" she asked.

"Where?" Marshall asked.

KC pointed. "See, on one of those arms."

"Yeah, I see 'em, but they're too small to read," Simon said.

"Wait a sec," KC said. She yanked open a drawer where Yvonne kept a lot of stuff. She pulled out a magnifying glass and held it over the cell-phone screen.

"They look like letters," Simon said. "The first one looks like a *D* or *O*, then *W*, *S*, and *n*. What's that spell?"

"Nothing," Marshall said.

"Weird," KC said. "Look, the first three letters are capitals, but the *n* isn't."

"Maybe it's part of someone's name," Simon suggested.

"Or a secret code!" Marshall added. "Maybe the green monster is really a spy who snuck into the party!"

Simon let out a laugh. "Or maybe he's from outer space," he said. "Maybe the guy's a Martian who came down to see how earthlings celebrate Halloween!"

Marshall grinned. "Yeah, and when his trick-or-treat bag is filled with goodies, he'll beam himself back up to Mars," he said.

They looked through the rest of Simon's pictures. There were a few more shots of the octopus holding a camera.

"I think the octopus took those pictures of the president, then changed them," Simon said. "All he'd need is a computer with the right software to put them on the Internet."

KC thought Simon was probably right. But what if he was just saying that to take the spotlight off himself?

"Anyway," she said, "we need to tell the president about the octopus with the camera."

KC and Marshall left the White House. KC knew the president was at campaign headquarters in the Washington Hotel. They hurried past the Treasury Department building and up the hotel steps.

KC led Marshall across the thick red carpeting of the lobby, past tall potted palm trees to a conference room around a corner.

"Oh my gosh," Marshall said as they walked into the room.

It seemed like a hundred people were dashing around, speaking into cell phones or carrying files of papers. Nobody looked happy. The only smiles in the room were on the campaign posters showing

President Thornton and Vice President Mary Kincaid.

Tables were jammed in wherever there was space. The tables held computers, telephones, bowls of campaign buttons, coffeepots, and trays of food. Men and women were using the computers and phones. The noise of dozens of voices filled the room.

KC counted six TV sets, all on. Each showed a different news channel. She recognized Donny Drum, but couldn't hear what he was saying.

Red, white, and blue bunting hung from the table fronts. Balloons in the same colors clustered at the ceiling. On one table, a chart showed how President Thornton and Dr. Melrose Jury were doing in the polls today. The line for Dr.

Jury was much higher than the one for Zachary Thornton.

"Can I help you kids?" a woman asked. Her hair looked as if she hadn't combed it in a while. Dark circles under her eyes made her look tired.

"Hi, I'm KC Corcoran," KC said. "Is the . . . is my stepfather here?"

The woman looked closely at KC. "Oh, of course," she said. "Sorry I didn't recognize you. This place is a madhouse today. He's in that office." The woman pointed across the wide room.

KC and Marshall walked around the tables, dodging volunteer workers and hopping over wires that lay on the floor like snakes.

The president sat at a desk speaking into a cell phone. His tie hung loose against his white shirt. As he talked, he was watching a small TV set. Like everyone else they'd seen, he had a grim expression on his face. Piles of pink message slips covered the top of the desk.

KC waited till he shut his cell phone, then she knocked on the door frame.

The president looked up. He smiled at his stepdaughter and Marshall. "Hey, come on in!" he said. "Got any good news? I could use some cheering up."

KC told the president about the Halloween guest in the green octopus costume.

"Yes, I remember him," the president said. "I thought he was some sort of sea monster."

"Marshall thinks it was Lauren Tool inside the costume," KC said. "He thinks she took those awful pictures of you."

"Lauren?" the president said. "I don't know, Marshall. I've known Lauren for a few years. In fact, I've hired her to take pictures in the White House before. I doubt she wishes me any harm."

"I think it might have been Simon," KC said. "He says he was taking pictures for a school report."

"And you don't believe him?" the president asked.

KC shrugged.

"I find it hard to believe that Yvonne's nephew would do such a thing," the president said. "I have a feeling that our camera culprit was inside that green costume. But I have no idea how he or she got past the marine guards and didn't pass through the tent like everyone else."

No one had an answer. Marshall told the president about the initials they saw on one of the octopus legs.

"D-W-S-N?" the president said.

"Or it might have been O-W-S-N, Marshall," KC added.

The president shook his head. He tapped the telephone. "Know who that was?" he asked. "My campaign manager. Those two pictures on the Internet have cost me fifteen points. Melrose Jury is ahead. Phone calls are coming in here and at the White House, and they're not very nice."

He stood up and looked at the two kids. "I might be the first president in history to lose an election because I gave a Halloween party."

5

The Disappearing Octopus

KC and Marshall walked back to the White House.

"We need to talk to the guards who worked at the party," KC said. "Maybe they saw the octopus guy sneak in or out."

"Unless the octopus was Lauren and she changed inside her tent," Marshall reminded her. "She could've slipped out the tent's back entrance and the guards wouldn't have known."

"Arnold might know who the three marines were," KC said finally.

KC expected to see Arnold standing in his usual spot, guarding the private residence. But he wasn't there. The marine who snapped to attention was shorter than Arnold. Like Arnold, he wore a crisp green uniform. His black shoes were so shiny they reflected the ceiling lights.

"Hi," KC said. "We were looking for Arnold."

"I haven't seen him today, miss," said the guard.

"But isn't this his usual post?" KC asked.

The marine shrugged. "My sergeant told me to report here," he said.

"Do you know which marines were on duty last night at the Halloween party?" Marshall asked.

"Sorry, I don't know that, either," the marine said. He smiled a little. "I'm not very helpful, am I?"

"Could I ask your sergeant?" KC asked. "Or whoever gives you guys your work assignments?"

"Sure," the guard said. "Check the guard hut outside the rear entrance." He looked at his watch. "Sergeant Royce should be there."

The kids thanked him and raced down the long hallway. Outside the back entrance, they headed toward the guard hut. It didn't really look like a hut. It was more like a small house, made of brick painted white. A path through a patch of lawn led to the hut. Rosebushes grew along the path.

Marshall stopped to admire a spider-web in one of the bushes.

"Marsh, we have to find an octopus, not a spider," KC said.

"It was here," Marshall said.

"What was here?"

Marshall plucked a strip of green plastic that had been hanging on a thorny branch. "The octopus," he said, holding up the fragment.

"What's that?" KC asked. "It looks like part of a green garbage bag."

"I think that's what it was," Marshall said. "But last night, this was part of the octopus costume. Remember those plastic strips that looked like seaweed?"

KC grabbed the piece from Marshall's fingers. It was about six inches long and one inch wide. "You're right!" she cried. "You can see where someone cut it with scissors!"

Marshall looked around. "No one from the party should have been way over here

by this guard hut," he said. "So why was the octopus here?"

"Maybe this is where he snuck in so he wouldn't have to go through the tent," KC suggested.

"Snuck in how?" Marshall asked. "He'd have to climb over an eight-foot-tall fence."

The door to the guard hut opened. A tall marine in a green uniform stood there. "Hi, Miss Corcoran," he said, recognizing KC.

"Hi, are you Sergeant Royce?" KC asked.

The marine smiled. "That's me," he said. His eyes narrowed as he noticed the strip of plastic KC held. "What have you got there?"

KC thought Sergeant Royce looked a

little too interested in this piece of plastic. She stuck it in her pocket. She was getting a funny feeling about this whole mystery.

"Um, we're working on something for the president," she said. "Do you know which guards were at the entrance to the Halloween party last night?"

"Sure," Sergeant Royce said. "Come on in and I'll check my duty roster."

KC had never been in the guard hut before. It was decorated like someone's living room, with chairs, a rug, and a TV in a corner. A large desk stood under an open window. KC noticed a jar of candy next to a laptop computer.

Sergeant Royce stepped over to the desk and picked up a clipboard. He flipped back a page and ran his finger down the sheet of paper. "Okay, there were three marines at the gate," he said. "Corporals Ditz, Henry, and West."

"Are they working today?" KC asked. "Can we talk to them?"

Sergeant Royce shook his head. "They're all off duty," he said. "They worked late last night cleaning up, so they get today off."

"Do you know where they are?" KC asked.

Sergeant Royce closed his eyes for a second. "I don't know about Corporal Henry," he said. "But I think Ditz and West took their motorcycles and went fishing."

The kids thanked Sergeant Royce and left the guard hut.

KC pulled the piece of green plastic from her pocket. "Did you notice the sergeant's face when he saw this?" KC asked Marshall. She waved the plastic strip.

"No," Marshall said.

"He looked like he'd seen it before," KC said. She glanced at Marshall. "Like maybe when it was part of an octopus costume."

"So . . . I'm confused," Marshall said. "How could he have seen the green costume? He wasn't one of the three guards on duty last night."

KC put the strip back in her pocket. "Maybe the octopus was Sergeant Royce," she said.

Marshall stopped walking. "Huh? Why would he want to make the president look bad before Election Day?"

"I don't know, Marsh," KC said. "It's

just a possibility. And I'm still thinking about Simon."

"But he told us he doesn't know how to put pictures on the Internet," Marshall said.

KC shook her head. "That's not exactly what he told us," she said. "Simon said his aunt's computer had crashed. He never said he didn't know how to do it."

The kids went back to the president's private apartment. Yvonne was in the kitchen brushing Natasha. The greyhound looked as if she enjoyed the attention.

"Hey, kids, what have you been up to?" Yvonne asked.

"Trying to find out who took those pictures of the president," KC said.

Yvonne finished with Natasha and gave her a doggy treat. "What a terrible thing to do," she said. "The vice president was just in here to get some juice. She said they've been getting phone calls all morning at campaign headquarters. And the polls have slipped even more. Right now, Melrose Jury is ahead."

"I know," KC said. "We just saw the president."

"We have to find the rat who took those shots," Marshall said.

The word *rat* reminded KC of why they'd come looking for Yvonne.

"I liked your costume," KC said. "And Simon looked great as Templeton the rat."

"Yeah, he was cute in it, wasn't he?" Yvonne said.

"Did he make the costume himself?" KC asked.

"I helped him put it together, but the

idea was his," Yvonne said. "I guess he found the costume online and went from there."

"Oh, do you have a computer at home?" KC asked innocently.

"I used to, but it broke down a few weeks ago," Yvonne said. "That's why I told Simon to bring his own laptop when he came to visit."

"Simon has his own computer?" KC asked. "Here, in the White House?"

"Honey, my nephew doesn't go anywhere without his laptop," Yvonne said. She brushed Natasha's silky ears. "He's constantly sending e-mails and pictures to his friends."

6

KC's Big Plan

KC dragged Marshall into her room and closed the door behind them. "Did you hear that?" she asked. "Simon has his own computer. I think Templeton the rat has been naughty."

"And I think Wilbur the pig is letting her imagination run away with her," said Marshall. "Again."

"Oh pooh," KC said. "Can you stay here for supper tonight? I have a plan. And I need you to help me."

"What kind of plan?" Marshall asked. "The kind where we end up in jail?"

KC grinned. "You heard what Yvonne said about Simon sending pictures. But he told us he couldn't send pictures! He lied, and I want to know why."

Marshall let out a hoot. "Oh, I get it," he said. "You're going to ask Yvonne to cook for us so we can get her nephew in trouble. Cool move, KC—really nice."

"Are you going to help me or not?" KC demanded. "I happen to know there's Choca-Moca ice cream in the freezer."

Marshall sighed. "Okay. The things I do for you!"

KC laughed. "The things you do for chocolate!"

Yvonne packed a picnic basket and handed it to Simon. Marshall carried a pitcher of red juice and glasses. KC followed with napkins, paper plates, and a blanket.

It was very warm for November. The sun had sunk below the trees, but there was still plenty of light on the lawn.

KC finished her first piece of chicken. She wiped her fingers on a napkin. "Your aunt told us you send a lot of e-mails to your friends," she said sweetly.

Simon had his mouth full, so he just nodded.

"She also told us you e-mail pictures," KC added. "But you told us you couldn't because Yvonne's computer was down."

Simon stopped chewing. His face turned as red as the juice on his lips.

"You forgot to tell us you brought your own laptop with you," KC went on.

Simon swallowed. "Okay, I lied about that part, so shoot me," he said. "I sent some pictures to my buddies so they'd believe I was hanging out with the president. But I didn't send any pictures like the ones on TV!" Simon stood up and threw his napkin on the blanket. "Someone else did that." He stomped away.

"Gee, that went well," Marshall said. He reached for another drumstick.

"Thanks for all your help," KC said.

"You did fine without me," Marshall said. "Now where's that Choca-Moca you promised?"

"Do you believe Simon?" KC asked. "I mean about not sending those pictures we saw on TV?"

"Yeah, I do," Marshall said.

KC collected the dirty napkins. "I believe him, too," she said quietly.

Just then they heard a loud engine roar on the other side of the hedge where they'd placed their blanket. KC stood on tiptoe and looked over the bushes. "It's Arnold on his motorcycle," she said.

"I want a motorcycle when I turn sixteen," Marshall said. He watched Arnold jog toward the guard hut, carrying his helmet. "Only I wouldn't wear a green helmet like his. It makes him look like a bug or something. I'd get a shiny red one."

"Oh my gosh!" KC yelled.

"Okay, maybe not red," Marshall went on. "Purple is cool, too."

KC grabbed Marshall by the arm and dragged him down onto the blanket.

"Marshall, listen!" KC hissed. "Think back to last night when we first saw the green octopus. There was something about that costume that wasn't right. Can you remember what it was?"

"Everything," Marshall said. "Plastic strips, stuffed arms that looked like green sausages, black shoes . . ."

"Yes! Shiny black shoes!" KC said. "Like marines wear here at the White House. Like Arnold wears every day."

"What made you think of Arnold's shoes now?" Marshall asked.

"Because I saw his green motorcycle helmet," KC said. "It was exactly like the one the octopus wore last night. That was Arnold in the green costume, and I just remembered his black shoes!"

Marshall stared at KC. "Arnold is the octopus?" he whispered.

KC nodded. Her eyes slid toward the guard hut. "I'd give anything to hear what he and Sergeant Royce are talking about."

"Well, you can't, so forget—"

KC stood up and grabbed Marshall's sleeve. "Come on, and stay below the hedge!"

"Where are we going?" he squeaked. "Oh, I know. I see jail time in my future. Who needs high school or college?"

With KC leading, the kids scooted from the hedge to the side of the guard hut. The window was too high for either of them to be able to peek inside.

KC looked around. She smiled when she spied a trash barrel. Using hand signals, she got Marshall to help her place it under the window.

Marshall held the barrel while KC climbed up and kneeled on the top.

Leaning against the building for balance, KC peeked through the screen. Arnold and Sergeant Royce were facing

each other, talking. Sergeant Royce's face was red. Arnold's face looked pale.

"Well, what's going on in there?" Marshall whispered.

KC turned to answer and the trash barrel tipped. KC fell off. The metal barrel clanged loudly as it hit the ground.

Sergeant Royce's face appeared in the window.

"What are you kids doing out there?" he asked. He sounded angry.

KC stood up and rubbed her bottom, where she'd landed hard. She couldn't think of a thing to say.

Marshall was frozen like a statue a few feet away.

"Please come in, Miss Corcoran and Mr. Li," Sergeant Royce said.

7

The Octopus Speaks

KC and Marshall walked around to the door. "Nice going," Marshall whispered. "KC, this reminds me of when Hansel and Gretel walked into the witch's hut."

Sergeant Royce opened the door. "Have a seat," he said. "I hope you like stories, because Corporal West has one to tell you."

KC and Marshall sat at the table across from Arnold. He was in full uniform, and his digital camera was on the table in front of him.

"I didn't know your last name was West," KC said to Arnold.

Arnold nodded. His face had gone

from pale yellow to pink, like a sunset.

Sergeant Royce sat in the remaining chair. He crossed his long legs. "Okay, get it off your chest, Corporal West," he said.

If KC hadn't been so upset, she would have laughed at the accidental poem.

Arnold took a deep breath. "I had forgotten all about the Halloween party until your mom asked me to bring the washtubs outside yesterday," he said to KC. "Then I saw Marshall's costume, and I got an idea. I went to my apartment and made a costume out of some of my old Marine Corps socks and a plastic garbage bag."

"An octopus, right?" Marshall asked.

Arnold blushed even deeper. "I know it was kind of lame," he said. "But it's the best I could come up with. I figured my motorcycle helmet would do for a mask."

Arnold stole a glance at Sergeant Royce. "The sarge assigned Ditz, Henry, and me to watch the gate," he went on. "After all the guests were inside, I asked Ditz and Henry to cover for me so I could come in here and get into the costume. Sergeant Royce was here, and he was nice enough to go along with it. See, I had my digital camera and I just wanted to get a few pictures of everyone dressed up."

KC nodded. "That's why my mom told us there were three guards at the gate, but Lauren Tool only saw two," she said.

Arnold looked at KC. "I planned to e-mail the pictures to my kid brother, Dez," he said. "After I took the pictures, I came back in here, got out of the costume, and went back to the gate. I was only gone about fifteen minutes."

"I'll take over, Corporal West," said Sergeant Royce. "I went along with West's idea to slip into the party, snap a few pictures, and slip out again. I saw no harm in it. But when I saw the pictures on TV, I knew something had gone wrong. And by the time you kids showed up earlier today, I knew the president was in trouble."

Sergeant Royce went on, "Corporal West was out of town fishing, and didn't see a TV or newspaper," he said. "He had no idea what was going on until I called."

"But the pictures showed the president dunking a kid and pinning a wart on Dr. Jury's face," Marshall said. "He'd never do those things!"

Arnold wiped his face with a dark green handkerchief he pulled from his pocket. "When I sent the pictures to my brother, he had an idea," Arnold said, shaking his head. "A really stupid idea."

"He changed the pictures, right?" KC said.

Arnold nodded. "Just for a laugh. He has this editing software that our father gave him for Christmas. It lets you change pictures and make new ones. Dez and I e-mail each other goofy pictures of the family all the time. He thought I'd get a kick out of seeing the president dunking a kid."

Arnold had a sick look on his face. "I never thought Dez would e-mail the pictures to his friends," he said. "I guess that's how they got all over the Internet."

Arnold wiped his forehead with the handkerchief again. Letters on the green cloth caught KC's eye.

"Could I see your handkerchief?" she asked.

Arnold handed it over.

"Look, Marsh," KC said. She put her finger on the initials *USMC*, for *United States Marine Corps.* Then she turned the handkerchief upside down. Now the initials were a backward *C*, then *W* and *S*, then an upside-down *U* that looked like an *n*.

"We saw the initials on one of the socks you used on your costume," KC said.

Sergeant Royce stood up. "Corporal West, you need to talk to the president as soon as he'll see you," he said. "For your sake, I hope he believes your story."

Arnold hung his head. "Yes, sir," he muttered. Arnold stood up and looked at KC. "I'd do anything for the president." Then he walked out of the guard hut.

8
Who Will Be President?

KC had a hard time getting to sleep that night. Every time she closed her eyes, she saw those fake pictures that showed the president doing awful things.

When KC finally slept, she had a nightmare. In the bad dream, the green octopus had been elected president.

KC woke up tangled in her blankets. She bolted up, thinking one of the octopus's tentacles had grabbed her.

But there was no tentacle wrapped around her foot. KC glanced at her bedside clock. It was almost eight o'clock. "Rats, I'll be late for school!" she muttered. Then she realized today was Sunday.

KC got dressed and walked to the kitchen. Simon was sitting at the table eating a piece of toast. His laptop was open, and he was pecking at the keys with one finger.

Yvonne was standing at the kitchen sink with her back to them. KC could tell that she was crying.

"Yvonne, what's wrong?" KC asked.

Yvonne turned around. She was holding a damp paper towel to her face. "The president was just here for his coffee," she said. "He told me I should think about looking for another job. He said he and you and your mom might be moving out of the White House after Christmas!"

KC sat down, stunned. She knew that when a new president moved into the White House, it happened in January.

"How could this happen, all because of a couple of pictures?" Yvonne went on.

Before KC could answer, they heard a knock on the kitchen door. Yvonne opened it to find Marshall standing there, out of breath. Behind him in the hallway stood Arnold, looking pale.

"I ran all the way," Marshall said. "Turn on the news. They're talking about the president."

KC turned on the small TV in the kitchen.

"This is Donny Drum, and I've got your news! Overnight, the president's poll numbers have gotten worse. With the election two days away, it seems certain that we will soon have a new president in the White House. Well, the candidates aren't talking, but we'd love to hear your comments! What do you think, viewers?"

Yvonne, KC, and Marshall stared at the TV set. No one moved.

"I have an idea," Simon said.

KC looked at him and turned down the volume. Marshall sat next to KC.

"We go see that Drum guy," Simon said, tipping his chin toward the TV. "We tell him we know exactly how those fake pictures got onto the Internet. We can bring him copies of the real pictures Arnold took. We'll tell him he'll be the only one with the real story, but he has to promise to put it on TV today."

KC shook her head, confused. "But it was Arnold and his brother," she said. "How do we—"

"We get Drum to put Arnold on TV, and Arnold can tell how his brother did it," Simon said. He looked at his aunt and grinned. "This will be huge. By tonight, the whole world will know the truth!"

KC nodded. "It's worth a try," she said. "Let's talk to Arnold." She jumped up and opened the kitchen door.

Donny Drum's Sunday-night story was so big it replaced the football games. KC, Marshall, the president, and Lois were watching it on the TV in the president's study. On the screen, Donny Drum was saying, "This is Donny Drum, and I've got your news!" He was interviewing Arnold and his brother, Dez West.

Dez looked into the camera and told the world how he had changed two innocent pictures. "I sent them to a couple of my friends," he said. "I thought that would be the end of it. I'd never do anything to hurt the president. Neither would my brother."

"So it was all just a joke among brothers," Donny Drum said, smiling into the camera. "What do you think of this, viewers? How will you vote on Tuesday? Should we keep President Thornton in office for another four years?"

When KC and Marshall walked into Thornton campaign headquarters with the president and KC's mom, three hundred people stood up and cheered. The computers and telephones were gone. In their place, the tables were covered with food and things to drink.

The sad and worried faces had also disappeared. Now everyone was smiling.

One woman was openly crying with joy.

It was Tuesday, November 4—Election Day. The clock on the wall said the time was nearly midnight. Most of the votes were in, all across the United States.

The president thanked his staff and volunteers. "It's not over yet," he said, trying hard to keep the smile off his face. "Dr. Jury could still win this election."

A large TV screen had been hung high on one wall. The volume was low, but one of the volunteers turned it up. Donny Drum's big white teeth grinned down at the room. Behind him were scoreboards showing that most votes had been cast for President Thornton.

"Well, you're seeing the same thing I'm seeing," Donny Drum said to his viewers. "It seems President Zachary Thornton will be our leader for the next four years. He has millions more votes than his opponent, Dr. Melrose Jury."

Someone handed Donny Drum a note. He read it quickly, then turned back to the camera. "Folks, I believe Dr. Melrose Jury has something to say to President Thornton."

Donny Drum's face disappeared. A different camera showed Dr. Jury picking up a telephone. Dr. Jury was smiling at the camera as he asked to speak to the president.

Just then a telephone on one of the desks rang. The president's campaign manager answered, then handed the phone to the president.

"Hello, Dr. Jury," the president said.

On TV, Dr. Jury said, "Congratulations,

Mr. President. I'm delighted that you'll be with us for four more years."

"Thank you, Dr. Jury," the president said. "I hope you'll come to the White House for lunch someday soon."

Dr. Jury laughed. "Can I have pizza?" he asked.

"I'll cook it myself," the president said.

When the president hung up the phone, the room erupted into whistles, clapping, and foot stomping. From large nets on the ceiling, thousands of red, white, and blue balloons began drifting down. Volunteers were hugging each other, tossing confetti into the air, and opening bottles of champagne.

KC's mom gave the president a big kiss, which got everyone whistling again.

KC and Marshall stuffed themselves

on cake and ice cream. They sat at a big round table with the president and vice president, Lois, Yvonne, and Simon.

"This is so cool," Marshall said. "We should have an election every year!"

"No way," the president said. "Every four years is plenty for me."

KC yawned. She closed her eyes and leaned against her mother.

"Hey, no fair going to sleep," Simon said from across the table.

"I wasn't sleeping," KC said. "I was just thinking about four more years of solving mysteries from inside the White House!"

Did you know?

George Washington was our country's first president. He was elected by the people. But as far as elections go, his were a breeze. Nobody ran against him! Very few  people voted, but every single vote went to George Washington in both 1789 and 1792.

Today, a person's vote is secret. It wasn't always that way. In some of the earliest elections, voters had to say their votes  out loud in front of everybody else. Over time, states began using paper ballots because they were easier to count. Also, the states hoped more people would vote if they could keep their choices secret. Voters cast their ballots by dropping a piece of paper into a box.

Each political party printed up a ballot with the names of its candidates. Then voters just used that ballot to vote. But since each party's ballot was printed on a different color paper, people could still tell who you were voting for!

The United States made a new kind of ballot. A blanket ballot lists all the candidates, and voters mark off the names of the people they want to vote for. All states now use blanket ballots, but the way of voting is still different from place to place.

Some states use big machines that record your vote when you pull levers next to candidates' names. In other places, you use a special computer to cast your vote. Some people mail in paper ballots. You may even still drop your ballot in a box!